THE BOY WHO DIDN'T FOLLOW DIRECTIONS

KATHY ZUZIAK

THE BOY

WHO DIDN'T FOLLOW

DIRECTIONS

By Kathy Zuziak

CITIOFBOOKS, INC.
3736 Eubank NE Suite A1
Albuquerque, NM 87111-3579
www.citiofbooks.com
Hotline: 1 (877) 389-2759
Fax: 1 (505) 930-7244

Ordering Information:

Quantity sales. Special discounts are available on quantity purchases by corporations, associations, and others. For details, contact the publisher at the address above.

Printed in the United States of America.

ISBN-13:   Softcover   979-8-89391-271-5
                  eBook   979-8-89391-272-2
                  Hardback   979-8-89391-270-8

Library of Congress Control Number: 2024916583

Table of Contents

This book is dedicated to Ella, who inspired me to write a story. She is dearly loved, and almost always follows the directions.

"The whole universe follows directions…"

The Owner

Chapter 1

Mrs. Keller's Problem

Marvin Pickles was usually a very smart boy. At video games he was amazing. He could slam his friend Tom at every game they played, like 600,000 points to 84,000, as an example. Okay, 84,750, in case he's reading this. Anyway, Marvin could figure out the rules and the short cuts really quick. That takes brains. And he was creative. He knew how to work around problems and to find alternate solutions, at least in the game world. He knew how to write stuff to look like 3D, which totally amazed his friend Amy, the girl that lived down the street and just so happened to be in his class at school.

Marvin thought Amy was cool. She had long, dark hair and always wore red sneakers. The only problem with Amy was that she was sick a lot. The doctors hadn't been able to figure out what was wrong with her. His mom said she must have some kind of autoimmune disease, like when the body attacks itself. Marvin didn't understand how that was even possible! If Amy wasn't at school, she was usually in the hospital. Marvin thought that must be tough and felt sorry for her.

So… back to Marvin being smart. He was usually a very smart boy…except for one thing. He didn't like to follow directions. (You can imagine that this would be a problem.) He didn't know why directions were such a big deal.

Maybe that's because his mom was a piano teacher, a real artist, and was big on creativity. "Think outside the box, honey," she always said. "Don't be like everyone else. Be unique. There's only one you!"

She gave a lot of piano lessons after school, right at the time when he wanted to tell her things, which was kind of annoying. He was proud of his mom, but wished he didn't have to share her with all those other kids.

It could be that, or…it might be that his stepfather was always telling him, "Do what you're told, son." And the trouble was he didn't want to be that guy's son. He wanted his own real father. Not that Henry was a bad guy, not really. He seemed to be trying. But he wasn't the same as a real dad. And Marvin was annoyed every time Henry implied that he was. So by association, "doing what you're told" was annoying as well. Couldn't everybody just leave him alone?

Marvin's problem was also a big problem for Mrs. Keller, his teacher. "Class," she would say, "Get out your science books and open to page 55." Marvin would take out a pencil instead, and draw in 3D or think up some imaginary scene where the pencil turned out to be some kind of alien torpedo. Usually very smart Marvin was not so smart at times like this.

Intelligence can be fickle, Henry always said. Apparently this was true.

"Follow directions, Marvin!" he would hear Mrs. Keller say faintly in the background, as if she were a dream.

Or "Class," she would say, "Please walk quietly in line." Instead, Marvin would shout to his friends and move however he wanted, shoulder to shoulder, or three feet away. Then the line would have to stop, and they were always late. Not smart.

It was like that all day sometimes. Smart, not smart. It made Mrs.Keller frustrated and sad to think Marvin wasn't learning like the other kids. Finally, she decided to do something drastic. She called…

THE MANAGER.

Chapter 2

The Manager

The Manager was only called in extreme cases. Mrs. Keller picked up her bright red cell phone. She told the Manager that Marvin's case was an emergency. The way he was going, he might not finish all his work like the other kids, and even though he was smart enough to pass, he'd have to do the same grade all over again!
THIS WAS AN EMERGENCY!

The Manager said she would come at once. Sure enough, just as soon as Mrs. Keller put down her phone, a woman walked into the classroom. She was dressed in a navy-blue business suit, and her hair, black with gray stripes, was pulled back and tied up in a bun. She wore big, round glasses and had a large nametag that read…

THE MANAGER.

The other kids watched curiously as she took Marvin aside and whispered into his ear. Then… the Manager…*and* Marvin… completely disappeared!

The other students were amazed. Billy Haverhill's mouth dropped open. They all looked at each other and wondered what she had said to Marvin, but it was too late. He was gone.

That day the class had the best learning afternoon they had in a long time.

Meanwhile, Marvin had his eyes shut tight. When he opened them, he was someplace else. It didn't look like home or anywhere close to home. The sun was not quite like the sun he was used to. It had stripes of red and looked sort of metallic-y. And the trees were definitely not trees he had seen before. They reminded him of a Dr. Seuss book. Even the texture of the dirt on the ground was not like home. It seemed like millions of tiny little dirt balls instead of just, you know, dirt. In the back of his mind he wondered if this might be another planet, but he dismissed that idea as too crazy. But wherever he was, he had gotten there FAST.

"And I didn't feel a thing!" he exclaimed.

"Well, you wouldn't," replied the Manager in a matter-of-fact tone of voice.

She pointed to a large sign that read…

DIRECTIONS GIVEN HERE.

"Do you see that sign, Marvin?" she asked. He nodded. "In this dimension you will be facing things you have never faced before. If you do not follow the directions, you will never make it."

The same thing happened as always happened with Mrs. Keller. The voice faded in the background like a dream.

Blah, blah, blah, it droned on as some gray, foggy sort of sound that had nothing to do with him.

Marvin was not listening. He was looking around at the funny shaped trees, and the odd surroundings, and then he made a rocket out of a stick from the ground, imagining how he might have arrived here. After a while, he noticed it had gotten quiet. He realized that the Manager had stopped talking. Then he looked up and he realized something else – he was

ALONE!

Chapter 3

Marvin Explores

"Hello?" he called out. No one answered. "I wonder where I am," he thought, and began to explore the area. He was a curious boy and always loved a challenge. Had he really heard the Manager say this was another dimension? What was it she was saying before she left? It was something about the sign. He tried hard to remember…well, sort of hard. But then, he saw a funny looking bird and his attention was totally consumed. He forgot all about the direction. Uh-oh, Marvin.

Not smart.

About lunchtime, according to Marvin's stomach, he began to get hungry. He looked around for an idea of something to eat. Although he couldn't tell what was food in this place, and what was not, he noticed an orchard of fruit trees not too far away. He walked over to it. Seeing something red and round hanging from the closest tree, he thought, "There's an apple!"

When he touched it, it fell into his hand, but when he bit into it, the fruit cried out, "Ouch!" Marvin immediately dropped it on the ground. The apple bounced away like it knew where it was going. So after his experience with the red object, he hesitated to try to eat things.

He left the orchard but continued to explore. Soon he found what seemed to him like a park with lots of trees, and right in the middle of the park was a silver slide. "This will be fun, " he thought, and ran over to climb on. He glanced around to make sure no one was watching, just in case it was only for the little kids, and then placed his foot on the bottom step. Before he was even halfway up the ladder, there was a loud siren blast and a gruff, gravelly voice shouted out, "Hey, YOU! Didn't you read the directions? You can't climb up that way! That's for climbing down! Somebody call THE MANAGER! This kid is out of control!"

Suddenly, the Manager stepped out from behind one of the trees and walked over to Marvin. The siren stopped blaring.

"What's the trouble?" she asked in a friendly tone. It was like she was looking right through him. He felt guilty without knowing why.

"All I did was try to climb up the ladder and…"

"You mean this ladder? Oh, no, no, no," she said. "In this dimension, we don't ever climb up the ladder. We climb down and slide up this part here," She pointed to the slippery looking sliding part."

"What? But …"

"Sorry, Marvin, the directions are…well, you know where they are. You might want to try following them. It will save you a lot of trouble." And with that, the Manager disappeared behind a tree.

Chapter 4

The Apple Explains

Marvin didn't feel like exploring any more. He was hungry and cross. "What did she mean I know where the directions are?" he thought grumpily. "This is a crazy place," he said and kicked a stone. Then he waited to see if it would talk. It didn't. He felt embarrassed about the loud siren and someone shouting at him. He wasn't feeling very smart and didn't like that feeling at all.

He just wanted to go home.

Marvin wandered around for a few minutes and finally found himself back where he started, at the orchard and the apple-that-you-couldn't-eat tree. Marvin gazed longingly at it, his stomach growling. While he stood there, an apple came bouncing close enough for him to touch. Marvin reached out, and then decided not to pick it up. He remembered what had happened the last time. Then something extraordinary almost knocked Marvin over. The apple spoke to him!

"You tried to eat me," it said in a hurt voice.

Marvin was shocked. The apple had TALKED to him. This was *definitely* not like home! A few seconds of silence passed. At last, Marvin remembered his manners.

"I - I'm sorry, " replied Marvin, "I didn't know you could talk."

"Well, I can," the apple sniffed, "Besides, everybody knows that. What's the matter with you?"

"How was I supposed to know? You look like an apple!" said Marvin, "At least where I come from."

"You didn't follow the directions," the apple sniffed again.

"You TOO? Is *everybody* a directions freak around here?" Marvin was starting to get upset. "What is this, the directions dimension or something?" He was feeling confused, and angry with himself for hurting the apple. So, as it sometimes happens, he lashed out at someone else to make himself feel better.

The apple was silent for a few seconds. Then he said quietly and calmly, "Actually, yes, it is in a way. This is the Organizational Dimension of the whole universe. We are the central map and information hub of the universe. Creatures come to us from all over the cosmos and from every dimension of time and space to get directions." Marvin had not expected an answer like that.

"Really? "Marvin asked unbelievingly. "Directions for what?"

"For EVERYTHING."

Chapter 5

Directions For Everything

The apple continued, "Directions are very important. Without them the flowers wouldn't bloom, the grass wouldn't grow, and the sun wouldn't shine. Don't you have directions in your dimension?"

Marvin thought awhile. Then he said, "Not for anything important, just school and stuff."

"Oh, school is very important in this dimension. In our school, the fruit learns when to ripen and when to fall off the tree. "

"Don't you just *know*?" Marvin was surprised.

"We know BECAUSE we follow the directions. "

"Well, what if you want to change the directions?" challenged Marvin. The apple tilted his head to look up at him. Marvin felt like he had asked a dumb question. The apple waited a minute, then said calmly, as if everyone should know this,

"The only one who can change the directions is the one who made the directions in the first place."

"Oh." Marvin sat down. He was tired and he was hungry. Suddenly he felt small, as small as an apple.

"Is there any *real* food around here?" he asked with his head down. His foot kicked at the dirt, making a dent.

"There is, but I'm not sure how to get it for you. You had better follow the, uh…," the apple paused and looked a little apologetic, "you know, *directions*." And with that advice, the apple bounced over to the huge sign that read,

DIRECTIONS GIVEN HERE.

"You'll have to wait in line, " the apple said helpfully. Sure enough, there was a line of creatures waiting to get advice for all kinds of different things. Marvin couldn't see who was giving the advice, but he thought it must be someone in the small booth behind the sign. Marvin HATED standing in a line. However, his stomach was *really* rumbling by now and he decided it was worth a try.

"Hey buddy!" snarled a large creature with pointy fins all over, "No cuts! Go to the end of the line!"

Marvin hadn't been going to take cuts and he might have tried to defend himself, but something happened to discourage him from doing that. A small brownish creature had stepped out of line for a second to scratch his fur.

Suddenly a very large, spiky, green animal barked, "No getting out of line!" and ate the small brownish creature in one gulp. Marvin did not get out of line once.

Chapter 6

Where Do You Want To Go?

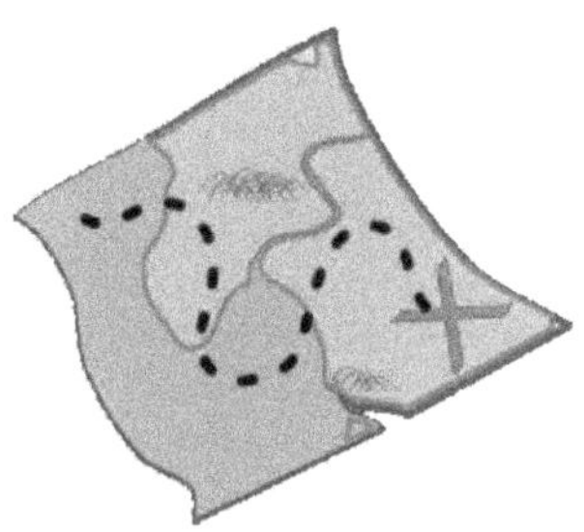

It was a long time before Marvin reached the front of the line. He heard a creature ask for advice on how to get to a friend's house. The friend lived 430 million light years to the left of the last planet in the Vooma galaxy. At least it *sounded* like "Vooma". He heard someone ask the way to a party! He heard the creature in front of him ask for directions to a planet in the 8th sector, whatever that was, and also for how to clean the asteroid dust off of his spacecraft. He heard one guy asking how to get to the theater and another the way to the beach. Also there were questions about what was polite in certain dimensions and what was rude. This question came from a creature missing an antenna and one eye. He had lost them in a fight. Someone had thought he was being rude.

When it was Marvin's turn, he looked up and saw a familiar face. The Manager smiled and asked, "How can I help you, Marvin? Where do you want to GO?" Encouraged by her smile, Marvin replied very truthfully, "I…I'm not sure.

I need something to eat and it's getting late. I should probably be getting home."

"You have come to the right place," she said and smiled kindly. "Directions given here," she pointed to the sign. "Where would you like to go first?"

"To find food I guess. "

"All you have to do is follow that road over there and it will take you to a tree with yellow fruit. Those are non-talking and safe to eat…. NEXT!" She turned to help the next creature in line.

Chapter 7

Apple's Problem

Marvin found the road and pretty soon he had a whole handful of tasty, yellow fruit. As soon as he had finished eating, he began to feel better. His friend the apple began to feel better too. They sat down on a funny-looking park bench and talked to each other about life in their different dimensions for a long time. Marvin forgot all about going home. And as they talked, it seemed to him that the apple was a lot bigger than it had originally appeared.

"I don't know why I ever tried to eat you", said Marvin. "I'm really sorry. You are WAY too big. It doesn't make any sense."

"That's ok, Marvin. Now that we are friends, things can't help but look different. You didn't *know* me." The apple made a fancy spin and bowed. Marvin laughed.

"They sure don't make apples like you where I come from."

Two large, purple pear-shaped things bounced by, nodding politely to the apple and Marvin. He figured they must be talking fruit. The apple was quiet for a second, trying to decide to say something.

"If I tell you something, will you promise not to laugh?"

"I promise," agreed Marvin solemnly, "But before you tell me that, tell me this. If you're not an apple what ARE you?" The apple smiled at him.

"I'm something like an am-am*phi*bian on your planet. You know, like a frog… although I'm only like a tadpole yet. You can call me Apple if you want to. I don't mind. I-I'm not sure you could pronounce my real name. It's a little tricky." Marvin gave an understanding nod and Apple took a big breath.

"I wanted to tell you," Apple took a gulp and continued. "There is a *dangerous* creature from another planet who comes here for directions sometimes. He REALLY tries to eat me. Last time, he nearly did! And he knows I'm a talking fruit. It's very bad manners. I guess that's why I'm a little sensitive," he sighed.

"That's TERRIBLE!" exclaimed Marvin. He was remembering the big, spiky green animal that ate things.

"The problem is," continued Apple, "he's *back*! I saw him in the line at the directions booth."

"WHAT?!" Marvin stood up, dropping the bite of yellow fruit he had been holding in his hand. "What are we doing sitting here out in the open? We should find a place for you to HIDE!"

The apple smiled.

"Thank you, my friend. You are so kind. I wanted to get to know you first. I was sure I was right about you, but…. it wouldn't be polite to…" Apple made a decision. "As it happens, I do know a place to hide, a safe house, but it is a long walk. Will you come with me?"

"Sure I will!" Marvin swept the last fruit pieces from his pants. "Let's get going before that …whatever it is… *finds* you!"

The apple nodded and led the way, bouncing as he usually did. Marvin couldn't help thinking it might be a good idea to put some distance between that creature and himself as well. He was feeling quite intelligent and responsible now. While they walked along, Marvin noticed something strange growing onto the apple's side, like a branch, but he kept it to himself, walking fast. They passed oddly-shaped houses and oddly-colored bushes. They walked around a wobbly pole stuck in the middle of the road. Marvin hardly noticed the funny-looking birds that sat on the pole peering down at him. He was on a mission to save his new friend!

On their way, they joked about the green spiky monster and Marvin nicknamed it Spike to help Apple feel better. It worked. Apple laughed. But just when things were going so well, Marvin's "smart – NOT smart" thing kicked in. It was the "not smart" thing that was the problem, of course.

"Don't step in that puddle," warned the apple. Marvin laughed, stepping directly into the middle of the puddle.

NOT smart!

Chapter 8

The Orange Ocean

He went down…all of him…down, down, down, into what seemed like a bottomless ocean and the ocean was not like the oceans at home. It was very, very ORANGE!

Marvin rolled around and around and around, orange bubbles exploding all around him, in his eyes, and nose and everywhere. Finally, he was able to get his bearings. He could open his eyes in the water and could see nothing but trouble ahead. A huge, scaly, dinosaur-like fish swam slowly underneath him. It hadn't yet noticed Marvin, but when it did…

TROUBLE!

Realizing his friend was in difficulty, the apple dove into the water to find him. There were now two appendages on his sides, and they helped him swim fast in Marvin's direction.

When the apple reached Marvin, the dinosaur fish was taking a leisurely glance around the area, probably searching for food. The good news was, the fish hadn't seen them. The bad news was, Marvin was running out of breath. The apple motioned for him to just relax and breath normally. Marvin was hesitant. This was a different kind of ocean, true...but breathe *under* water? Then he saw the apples new arms and figured ANYTHING was possible in *this* place. He closed his eyes and took a breath.

Wow! He couldn't believe it. He was breathing! UNDER water!

This was amazing! He turned a somersault and then another. He flipped and flopped and twisted and dove, never needing to come up for air. He wished he could swim forever! This is how it must feel to be a fish!

Meanwhile, Apple was anxiously trying to get his attention. He was pointing to the giant fish below, who at any MINUTE was going to SEE them! Then he would open his giant JAWS so they could see his MILLIONS of giant teeth!

But Marvin was enjoying his swim too much to notice. Apple tried harder, swimming in one spot with all his might. He motioned frantically to Marvin, pointing down. Marvin saw the motion and at the same time did a flip. While he was upside down, he also glanced in the direction of the monstrous fish and saw two big monstrous eyes staring right up at him! Trouble with a capital T! Here came the fish, jaws open wide, hoping to swallow Marvin and Apple in one giant gulp.

LOOK OUT!

The next thing Marvin knew, he was being pulled, vacuumed up and up until he was out of the water, lying on the road next to the puddle he had jumped into. He didn't know how or who or what or why, but he was not eaten by the monster fish. He was shaking, and not from the cold. That was too close!

He tipped his head and tapped some water out of his ear and looked around for his friend the apple. Apple was sitting a few feet away from the puddle, flicking water drops from his shiny red skin.

"What *happened*?" Marvin almost shouted. "The last thing I remember was we were fish food!"

"I didn't see, but it was probably the Manager that pulled us out of the water."

"The Manager? She's not even here!" He was shivering.

"Well…she's pretty fast. You'll get used to it." Apple said, forcing a half-hearted smile.

"Wow, no one back home would believe I was breathing UNDER water. That's the coolest thing ever!" Marvin got to his feet, but then as he thought about his narrow escape, his legs began to feel like jelly. "We'd better get you to that safe place," he said to Apple in a more sober tone.

"Yes," Apple agreed, looking worriedly over his shoulder, "I have a bad feeling. I think Spike is looking for me."

Marvin straightened his wobbly legs and whispered, "Let's go!"

Chapter 9

An Awkward Silence

They walked and bounced along for a while. Neither felt like talking. Marvin was thinking about things. Who was this Manager? Was she watching out for him? Did she watch out for everybody? Or was she SPYING on him? Was she watching, waiting for him to mess up again?

Apple glanced sideways at Marvin. He wanted to say something, but changed his mind and shook his head. They went over an odd-looking stone bridge and looked down at the river flowing below. There were a few multi-colored leaves drifting and swirling on the top of the water, close enough to poke at with a stick, but somehow Marvin didn't feel like playing in the water now. He thought of his friend Amy and how she would have loved to see all these things. She probably would have brought her camera and would be taking pictures of everything. And of course, he would say it was a dumb thing to do, when really, he thought it was cool. Mostly, he wondered why Apple was so quiet. It bothered him that no one was saying anything. It was an awkward kind of silence.

"Apple, are you all right?" Marvin asked finally. It was a relief to break the silence. Apple nodded his big red head and Marvin noticed the head seemed to be dented in spots. He didn't say anything about that, not wanting to draw attention to it in case Apple would feel uncomfortable, but he did want to know one thing. "Why is Spike after *you*? I mean personally. Is he just looking for any apple or just you?

"Just me," Apple sighed. Then his mouth curved in a half smile. "I fell on his head once." Marvin giggled. Then Apple giggled. "He howled and howled and then he didn't watch where he was going and stepped in a hole. It took him a long time to pull his big foot out and everyone was laughing. I guess he's the kind of creature who holds a grudge." They both laughed. Then Apple got serious. "He searched for me for hours that time, sniffing the air to follow my scent. That's when I found the safe house."

"Are we getting close?" Marvin asked, as they continued walking.

"Yes. Just over this hill is a meadow of flowers. You can smell them from here."

"Oh, yeah! I smell them. Mmmm, what a great smell! It's like cotton candy back home…no, wait…cinnamon… and…and chocolate! COOKIES!!"

"Be careful when you get close to them. They imitate the smells you like but you can't eat them, not even one bite."

"What happens if you do?" Marvin asked.

"You'll die. They're POISON!"

Chapter 10

The Blue People

A few moments later they were facing a GYNORMOUS field, a multi-colored carpet of the most beautiful flowers Marvin had ever seen in his life. Every hue, every color was dotted here and there like fruit loops with thin, dark green leaves. Apple bounced into the midst of them shouting, "Come on!" But Marvin stood still, breathing in the delightful aromas. He took big whiffs and tried to hold them in as long as he could, savoring each yummy smell. Oh, if he could only taste them! *How could they be poison and smell that good?*

"Marvin, where are you?" Apple called and still Marvin seemed rooted to the spot. There was a thumping noise not too far away, in a dream it seemed. It smelled so wonderful…

"He's COMING!" shouted Apple, "Spike is HERE! Snap OUT OF IT, Marvin!" At those words, Marvin blinked and shook his head to clear his mind. The dream had to become a reality right now!

"Marvin! He's behind you! LOOK OUT!!" Apple cried.

"DIVE!"

Something pushed him, Marvin said when he told the story later on, or he would never have made it. A second, no, a *micro*second after he dove into the flowers, the huge, lopsided head of the green, spiky monster appeared over the hill. He was feeling hungry and looking for Apple (or anyone else to have for dinner).

Marvin lay perfectly still, face down on the ground, nose to the dirt, flowers standing tall all around him, shielding his body from the eyes of the creature they laughingly called Spike. There was no laughing now. He hardly dared to breathe

"Pssst! Earth boy!" came the hushed voice. He turned his head carefully, quietly, low to the ground, to find where the voice was coming from. Then he heard the CRASH! STOMP! THUD! THUMP! SNORT! SNIFF!

The monster creature had stepped into the field of flowers, just a few yards from where Marvin lay, trying again to be rigidly still, yet searching to see who had whispered to him.

His eyes rested on the source of the voice. It was a tiny creature, like a toy soldier, *all* blue, that had called him. The little blue figure was motioning for him to come. He seemed very sure that he wanted Marvin to follow and it looked to him like the little man, if that's what it was, wanted him to crawl over to…WAIT! Now he saw them!

There were tiny houses or shelters of some kind built right into the stems of the flowers! They were like tree houses, except miniature in size. Marvin was fascinated. You couldn't see them if you were standing, but lying on ground with his eyes at insect level, he had a whole different perspective on things.

The little blue man was motioning for him to come inside the tree house. Well, that was a nice invitation, but Marvin was a giant compared to the size of the tree house. How would he ever fit? SNIFF! SNORT! STOMP! SNIFF-SNIFF! The creature was coming closer, smelling and sniffing at the flowers, and would find Marvin very soon if he didn't do something FAST!

The blue man pointed to the tree house. Marvin saw something move in the tree house and strained hard to see what it was. It was really, really small, but Marvin thought he saw Apple waving at him, inside the house! Apple had SHRUNK to the size of the blue man!

The blue man was almost jumping up and down now, insisting that Marvin come at once. SNIFF! SNORT! Marvin crawled slowly toward the tree house. When he reached the little blue man, he was surprised that the man had grown. And how it happened, he never knew, but as Marvin thought about stepping inside the tree house, there he was, no problem! Incredible! Tom would never believe it! Amy would never believe it! Billy Haverhill would never believe it. But it was true.

Chapter 11

The Safe House

When Marvin saw Apple sitting on the porch, he was shocked. Apple had grown two thin legs to go with the two arms growing now out of his sides. That must have been what those dents were, he thought. What was going on? And there were blue people all around, here and there, going about their business, for this was their home. Not this particular tree house, but the whole tree house "city." Marvin could see now that there were many others like this one, all built into the sides of the flower stems. Every time the flower would bend or sway in the breeze, the tree house would bend or sway with it, sort of in a slow-motion movement. And if you watched for a while, all the tree houses did the same. It looked like they were dancing.

He turned to Apple.

"What is this place?" he asked.

"The safe house," Apple replied. He stretched his legs, "Do you like them?" he asked, referring to his new body parts.

"Of course, Apple, but how did this *happen*? Where did they come from?" He hadn't thought too much about

Apple's arms growing. Everything was all so strange in this dimension. But Marvin was SUPER curious about the legs. What could cause an apple to grow arms and legs? And what would grow next? Would he, Marvin start growing arms and legs? Not knowing made him nervous.

"Sh!" warned one of the blue men. Marvin wasn't sure if it was the same one who spoke to him before or not; they all looked so much alike. But he stayed quiet.

Nobody spoke or moved. There was no sound except for the gentle breeze that caused the tree houses to sway. The blue man had his finger on his lips. It must be a universal sign for quiet, thought Marvin. Then he realized what they were listening for. Spike was not thrashing around, sniffing anymore. If that was true, then what was he *doing?*

All of a sudden, there was a BOOM! And a THUD! And finally a THUMP! One of the blue men motioned for Apple and Marvin to come into the inner room of the house. There they discovered what looked like at least twenty blue men, all monitoring computer screens with different views of the flower field on them. THIS was why it was a safe house, Marvin realized. These were security monitors to protect the tree house people. On four of the screens, there was a picture of Spike, from different angles, lying face down in the flowers.

"He's dead," sighed one of the blue men, "We are all safe."

"But what happened?" Marvin asked. "How did he die?" He was certainly relieved, but confused, and was still shaking on the inside from hearing the last THUMP. That had been another close call – for all of them.

"He ate the flowers instead of us," Apple explained. "I *told* you they were poison." Marvin thought how close he had come to tasting one and gulped. Thank goodness he had followed *that* direction!

Chapter 12

An Enemy?

Apple was looking sad. Marvin followed him out of the monitor room and back to the porch, where they sat gazing out at the tree house city. It was that uncomfortable silence again. Something was bothering Apple. Marvin hated not knowing, but he was embarrassed to ask. Instead, he dug his toe in a little crack on the ground and twisted it to see if the crack would get any bigger. It didn't. Finally, Apple decided to speak.

"Can I ask you a question, Marvin?"

Relieved, Marvin nodded enthusiastically. "Sure, Apple, what is it?" His friend frowned and slowly flexed first one leg and then the other one.

"I have to know, Marvin. Are you… the ENEMY?" The question shot out like a bullet and went straight to his heart.

"Wh-what are you talking about, Apple? I'm not your enemy. I'm not *anyone's* enemy."

"Think about it, Marvin. You deliberately sunk us in the Orange Ocean, almost got us eaten by that, that FISH!"

"That wasn't *my* fault! It was an accident! I didn't know that ocean was even there!"

"But I *told* you not to step in the puddle and you didn't follow my direction."

"Well I…" Marvin stopped the excuse that was coming so quickly out of his mouth. He had a flashback and remembered. Apple was right.

Then Apple continued, "And when we got to the flower field, I told you to follow me and dive into the flowers, but you stayed and stayed until the monster could see you. You led him right here, didn't you?" Apple was looking at him, brand new arms folded, a frown on his face, as if Marvin WAS the enemy.

"Why did you do it, Marvin? I thought we were friends." Then Apple turned away and wasn't looking at him anymore.

Marvin was stunned. All of those things Apple said were true. He didn't know what to say. "I - I…Apple, I didn't MEAN to cause those things to happen. It was an…"

"An accident, Marvin?" Apple whirled around, finishing the sentence for him. "How can you say that? I *told* you what to do!"

Marvin sat very still. His mind was trying to make sense of it all. If what Apple said was true, then he, Marvin had been a big dope and placed them in a lot of danger for nothing. Smart - not smart changing its fickle mind again. No wonder he had been accused of being the ENEMY! If he had just done what Apple had said to do none of this might have happened. And now Apple was looking so sad, Marvin couldn't stand it! The words just came spilling out fast before he could stop them. He stood up and faced his friend.

"Apple, listen. I don't know why it's so hard for me to follow directions. It gets me in trouble all the time. You were right about everything, except the part about me being an enemy. I wouldn't hurt you for anything!" There! He said it and felt relief. These were things he had never told anyone, but Apple needed to know.

In fact, the things Marvin had admitted made all the difference to Apple. He wasn't sad anymore. His face had softened.

"I would never hurt you either, Marvin," he said. This time the silence was not uncomfortable. It was kind of peaceful.

"Marvin, I bet the Manager could help you understand why it's so hard for you to follow directions," Apple said, breaking the silence. "Let's go ask her." And before Marvin could even reply, Apple had grabbed his arm and was leading him off the porch. In two seconds they were normal size again, hurrying back through the field of flowers, and on their way back to the information booth.

Chapter 13

Let Me In!

Again there was a line. Marvin went to the end and waited patiently for his turn. Apple waited patiently for Marvin. His eyes travelled down his new arms and new legs and over his body that was becoming thinner. He was grateful to Marvin. Without this boy's help he would never have been able to go through the metamorphosis.

When Marvin reached the front of the line there was a different person giving information. He was a short little man with frizzy red hair. He also wore big glasses.

"Where's the Manager?" asked Marvin nervously.

"She's taking an emergency call." The little man was very serious. "Where would you like to go, young man?"

"I'd like to go home, sir," replied Marvin. "But first, I need to talk to the Manager about why it's so hard for me to follow directions. Maybe she can help me."

The little man scratched his head, rubbed his nose, then said, "Hmmm. I'll have to look that up. You'd better come in. You can use the side door."

Marvin peeked around the corner and, sure enough, there was a door in the side of the information booth. He turned the handle, but it was locked. He knocked and waited, but no one came. He knocked again and tried to speak loud enough for the man inside to hear.

"I can't open the door! I'm trying but it's locked or something! "

"Pipe down, you! There's no loud talking around here!" a very fat, wobbly creature complained. There was a rustling sound as if the creatures in line were moving restlessly.

"Hey, Pete! Don't those line directions say no loud talking? I thought they did."

Someone else remarked quietly, "Everyone knows that, don't they?" There was an underlying sound of a growl, then another, and it was growing in intensity.

"Who's the wise guy not following the LINE DIRECTIONS?" Marvin began to get VERY nervous. He was thinking about the small, brown creature that had been Spike's snack. There might be other Spikes out there. He yanked on the doorknob, pulling with all his might.

"Please let me in!" he whispered, beginning to panic. It sounded like some of the creatures were coming around to the side and they would surely find him, and maybe eat him! Marvin pulled on the door handle again as hard as he could.

"Let...ME... IN!!"

Just in time, the door flew open and the little man was standing there, in a white lab coat, motioning quickly for him to come inside.

Chapter 14

The Center–of–It–All

He was in and the door closed behind him. Marvin stood and gazed in amazement at what he saw. It was like another WORLD. The room was quite large, huge really, like a factory or warehouse, yet gave the impression of a library or an antique shop. It was filled with all kinds of objects as well as old books, a vast array of maps, globes, clocks, very old machines with lots of turning gears, and a team of what appeared like researchers dressed in white lab coats so that they looked like scientists or doctors. These researchers were busily engaged in working, studying maps, setting clocks, reading and thumbing through books, and a number of other things that Marvin didn't know anything about.

In addition to the past, there was also the present and the future represented, with things like holograms, and tiny, flying objects zooming around virtual computer screens in the air. Here there was everything imaginable and unimaginable.

"This is highly irregular, you understand. No getting around it, I will have to summon the Manager. " The little man took a small, watch-like object from his pocket and gave the top a twist. Before he could blink, Marvin was face to face with the Manager. How did she DO that?

She looked kindly at him, and swept her hand out in front of her as an invitation to admire the surroundings and then said, "Welcome to the CENTER–OF–IT–ALL, Marvin. This is where ALL directions come from! You may go, Porter, I'll take it from here." The little man hurried away.

Marvin was amazed at this room. He looked back at the door he had come in and wondered why the inside didn't look anything like this from the outside. How was this possible?

"Does *everybody* know about this?" he asked.

"Oh, no, Marvin" she replied, shaking her head solemnly. "Only a very, very few. " This made Marvin feel suddenly strangely happy. He was one of the privileged few.

"Come with me, please, " she said and walked quickly around the maze of obstacles, desks, chairs, and people in white. Marvin followed, slowing to look at all of the interesting objects, and then hurrying to catch up. The room was so large he thought it would go on forever, but after a while they stopped abruptly at a door. The door was made of some kind of metal, a bit rusty, and it looked like some of the dark green paint had been scratched off near the handle. It didn't look very impressive. In fact, it seemed rather shabby.

The Manager opened the door and somehow, although there wasn't any light switch, a turquoise-colored light began to glow dimly around the walls of this small room.

"This is the game room," said the Manager. "Here we keep the scores and the replays of everyone's game. Marvin blinked a couple of times. He loved games!

"What game?" He tried to imagine. Football? Soccer? A video game? Monopoly?

"Can I play it?" he whispered, almost to himself. Now he was getting excited. Games were something he was good at.

"Can I play it?" he asked again, louder this time.

"You *are* playing it, Marvin. You're playing it right NOW."

Chapter 15

Marvin's Game

"Your *game*, Marvin, is your LIFE." Let's watch a replay of five years ago." The Manager motioned for him to sit down in a very uncomfortable-looking, metal chair. She did not sit. She picked up a clipboard, pushed a button on the wall that Marvin couldn't see, and a very large, shiny, silvery white screen appeared in front of them. A video began to play, and as Marvin watched, he began to recognize some of the scenery in the film.

"That's *my* house!" he cried, and jumped up to touch the screen. Unfortunately, the screen was not really there and his hand went right through the hologram. Marvin lost his balance and almost fell, feeling foolish. He settled back into his chair and saw the action play out on the screen as if he had been a character in a movie. He saw a younger version of himself ride off on a bike and heard his mother call, "Keep to the right!" The next scene was Marvin, sprawled on the ground, crying.

"What happened?" he asked the Manager. "I kind of remember falling, but I don't remember why."

The Manager glanced at her clipboard, flipped a page, and then said, "Ah." She pointed to the page. "You didn't follow the direction your mother called out to you and you rode to the *left*. There was a piece of cement sticking up on the ground. It caused you to fall. You didn't see it, but your mother did."

"Oh," said Marvin.

"We will go back two years." There were some squiggly purple lines on the screen and suddenly there was Marvin, playing baseball. His team was in the outfield and he was playing in close, almost right next to the second baseman. His coach yelled for Marvin to move out farther. The movie Marvin stayed where he was. The real Marvin cried, "Move back! MOVE BACK!" Then came the sound of a crack and the ball was flying right toward him. Marvin started to move back but he was too slow. The ball whizzed over his head and by the time he ran to get it, the batter had rounded first base, heading for second. The other team was heard cheering in the background. The throw to second was missed and the batter ran on to third.

Marvin moaned, putting his hand on his forehead. "Why didn't I move back? I could have caught that ball. We missed the playoffs because that guy scored."

"Didn't you *hear* the coach?" the Manager asked curiously.

Marvin didn't answer. Now he remembered. Of course he had heard the coach. He just thought he knew better and didn't want anyone telling him what to do. Touching the arm of the chair, Marvin drew a circle on the metal. He was remembering the look on his stepfather's face that day. It had been curiously sympathetic. Marvin had forgotten about that.

"Let's go back one year," said the Manager. The screen again showed squiggly purple lines and then a hospital scene exploded into view. Doctors and nurses were bustling around and there was a patient lying on a bed, eyes closed. It was a girl with long brown hair, and she looked very sick.

"That's Amy, " Marvin said in a surprised voice. "What's wrong with her, Ma'am?"

The Manager checked her clipboard. "She has contracted the flu again."

"Oh, is that all? I had the flu once, but I didn't have to go to the hospital for it."

"Amy has an immune system disorder. To her the flu is more dangerous because her body can't fight it off like yours can."

"That's awful," said Marvin sadly. "She should be careful not to get sick." He twisted uncomfortably in his chair. He was picturing the day when he went to play at her house. Was *that* the day he had stayed home from school because he had had a fever?

The Manager looked down at him. "Your mother gave you a direction that day, Marvin. Do you remember?"

He didn't want to remember. He liked Amy. She was cool. There was a silence that was thick and dark.

Finally he confessed. "She told me not to go near Amy until I felt better." He wanted to crawl under the chair. "But she didn't tell me *why not*."

"Grownups don't always tell why or why not because that is their direction. They are following directions THEMSELVES."

Chapter 16

Directions for Grownups

"What do you mean?' Marvin asked, suddenly starting to get VERY interested.

"Grownups are given a *big* responsibility," explained the Manager. Grownups CARRY the directions and give them to the children. They may sometimes answer questions about the directions like "why" or "why not," but many times they are not allowed to tell. The children need to follow the directions anyway. That is what helps make them grow."

"I thought food made you grow," said Marvin, feeling that dinnertime should be getting close. He tapped a rhythm on the side of the chair.

"No, " replied the Manager. "It is the directions that make you grow. The body is just following directions too, directions to use the food you eat."

"Oh." He thought about this as the silver screen offered numerous purple squiggles for his viewing enjoyment.

And then, the scene was his classroom. Mrs. Keller was standing at the front of the room saying, "Class, please turn to page 55 in your science book." Marvin remembered hearing those words, but he was surprised to see himself ignoring his teacher like that. He saw everyone else turn to the right page and saw himself pick up a pencil and play with it. He was embarrassed. Marvin heard Mrs. Keller ask him again to open his book and then he saw the pencil go flying in the air. The other students were distracted. Marvin could see that now. Mrs. Keller took the pencil and told Marvin to sit in a desk away from the other children. Again, he felt embarrassed that the Manager was seeing what he was seeing. To think that just a short while ago, he had been feeling so responsible. Intelligence was certainly fickle *that* time, Henry would say. I guess Henry was smarter than Marvin had thought. He kind of wished Henry was here now.

"Marvin, where did Mrs. Keller want the class to GO?"

"Page 55," he said quickly. He knew now.

"Page 55 is just the beginning," the Manager told him. "Mrs. Keller wants the class to read the words and see the pictures so that they will learn the information… so they will know things, so that they will get a good score on the test… so that they will pass this grade… so that they will grow up to be successful and happy people. There are so MANY reasons, many "whys" and "why nots" that she is not telling you. She has been following her directions and you, Marvin… have not. Can you tell me why or why NOT?"

Chapter 17

Why Not?

Marvin couldn't think of a reason exactly. That is, one that sounded reasonable. Isn't this why he came to the Manager, for her to help him find out why not? The Manager waited for a minute and then broke the silence.

"There is one more scene that I want you to see," said the Manager. The screen went all purply again and then it was dark. Marvin couldn't see anything. Instead of shouting out," I CAN'T SEE ANYTHING!" he decided to be patient and wait for the Manager to fix the screen. She didn't. Instead, a strange siren sound seemed to be coming from the screen. There was movement, but it was so dark Marvin couldn't make out a person or a place. Then the background grew a little bit lighter and finally he could tell that the darkness was SMOKE, big black smoke all around a house. No wonder he couldn't see!

There were fire engines and police cars and an ambulance all arriving at the scene. Sirens, hoses, water, and firemen all contributed to the confusion. What had happened? Marvin didn't remember any of this taking place.

Then he saw his little sister lying on the ground. Grownups were all around her trying to revive her. She must have been breathing the smoke. Marvin's eyes darted wildly back and forth trying to find his parents in the crowd on the screen.

The fire chief was talking with one of the grownups. He was saying that the fire started in the little girl's bedroom.

"What!! No! I would never start a fire! I always tell my sister not to play with matches! I always tell her…" He stopped right then.

The Manager said softly, "Go on, Marvin. What direction do you always give your little sister?"

Marvin was thoughtful. It was all starting to make sense in some crazy way. Grownups followed directions and gave them to him. He was supposed to follow directions and give them to his sister, or someone younger than him.

"*Everything* follows directions, Marvin. The clouds to make rain, the rain to water the earth, the earth to make rivers, the rivers to provide water for fish to live in and for you to drink. Do you understand what is going on?

Marvin nodded, "Better now. I used to think that directions were just grownups trying to boss me around and tell me what to do. I didn't think it *mattered*. So I guess I just tuned it out." He looked up at the Manager who was smiling at him. " I guess I was wrong."

"I guess so," she said kindly. "Take some time, Marvin, to think. It will help you." She quietly left the room and closed the door behind her. Marvin was left alone with himself.

Chapter 18

Marvin Understands

He was thoughtful…and then horrified! There was no denying he had been wrong. No WONDER his friend Apple had accused him of being the enemy! He had put others in DANGER by not following the directions. Like Amy… and Apple… and of course, himself. How many close calls had he had today? Too *many*!

He sat in the cold metal chair, poking its arm with his finger. He felt like a big dork and was mad at himself. He wondered how many others had seen the video of his life and all the dumb choices he had made. He wished he could erase it and start over. Then at least Amy wouldn't have gotten so sick. Would she forgive him if she knew the truth? He didn't know. Could he ever forgive himself? And what about his sister? He had to get back and see if she was really all right.

The hologram was still showing the purple lines, and there was a faint scratchy hum sound coming from some speaker somewhere.

Marvin wasn't sure, but he thought he saw some movement on the screen. No, it just sort of lost focus and then the lines were back. Wait, there it was again. Something was trying to come into view. He couldn't see it clearly. There! He tried to move his chair closer, but it was heavy and didn't move much. Marvin heard a faint sound like a radio voice coming into range. Then it was clear. He was watching himself in a movie again.

The scene was the auditorium at his school. Everyone was there, including his parents. The principal was speaking at the podium up on stage and there was Marvin walking up to the platform. What was going on? He didn't remember this!

As he watched, the principal shook his hand and gave him some kind of paper or certificate or something. Suddenly, the sound became crystal clear.

"For outstanding bravery and following the police officer's directions, you saved three children and helped capture a dangerous criminal. Marvin Pickles, on behalf of the whole school we award you this honor. Congratulations, Student of the Year!" Everyone was standing and applauding. His mom and Henry were beaming with pride. Then the screen went blank.

Wow. Wouldn't that be the coolest thing? Marvin thought about it for a while. He had followed the policeman's directions and saved some kids. Really? Him? Was that the real future or just a future that *might* happen?

I guess directions are a *good* thing, he said to himself. Maybe they are a REAL good thing!

The door opened and the Manager came in. She looked at Marvin with that seeing-right-through-him look. His eyes moved from the floor up to the screen and then up to look confidently right in the Manager's eyes.

"I think I get it now," he said.

"I think you do too, " she smiled. "Always remember Marvin. Following directions will help you get to where you want to go. WHEREVER that might be."

He nodded.

"I'll remember." There was a pause. Then he asked, "Ma'am?"

"Yes, dear?" the Manager replied, sounding less businesslike and more mom-like.

"Is my sister ok?" She nodded.

"She has you to protect her." Marvin felt very grownup. He couldn't wait to tell Apple everything.

Chapter 19

Apple's Story

When Marvin saw Apple again, he almost didn't recognize him. Apple had become a normal-looking BOY! His head was a bit large and round, like an apple, of course, but he had two arms, two legs, and his body had slimmed to a proper proportion for a boy's body.

"Well, what do you think, Marvin? How do I look?"

"Apple? Is it really you? I can't believe it! You look like a regular kid! You have arms and legs and, and *everything*!

"It's all because of you, Marvin," Apple said.

"WHAT?" Marvin said. " *I* didn't do anything. You just changed! I saw you!"

"That's because you let me help *you*," Apple replied.

Marvin scratched his head.

"Wait a minute, Apple. Wasn't I helping you? " Apple shook his round head.

"Yes I was, " Marvin argued. "You *asked* me, remember? We were talking and you…"

"Sure, Marvin, you did agree to help me and as you see…" Apple took a flourishing bow, "It has helped me very much. I have been able to complete my metamorphosis and I have you to thank for it."

"But how did it happen? I did everything wrong." Marvin couldn't stop staring at Apple's new body. It was simply the coolest thing he had ever seen. EVER!

"The way it works for my species is that when we help someone else, we are able to grow, not in size, but to a new level of maturity, you might say. Each time I was able to help you in some way, it provided me with an opportunity to grow or change. And I'm *loving* the new me!"

"I like it too, Apple. Wow, Amy will *never* believe this! Maybe we could ask the Manager and I could take you home with me. Then she'd HAVE to believe it!"

"Mm-hmm," Apple agreed half-heartedly, looking over Marvin's head toward the orchard.

"Let's go ask for directions, Apple. Come on!" Marvin grabbed his friend's arm, and they ran until they came to the line at the Directions Booth. This time, Marvin was happy to wait in line and it was no time at all until he was at the window.

"Can Apple come home with me, Ma'am?" asked Marvin rather breathlessly. She looked at him and then at Apple.

"I'm afraid not, dear," she said kindly. "Apple has work to do here and his family needs him."

"His *family*?" Marvin was shocked. He had never considered the possibility that Apple could have a family. Turning to look now into Apple's eyes, he said, "Where is your family, Apple?" His friend pointed.

"Our tree is over there, where you first met me." Apple was looking sad.

"What's wrong, Apple? Are they all right?" Marvin was genuinely interested. He felt good about that too. Maybe *he* had "metamorphed," or whatever you called it, like Apple.

"There are a lot of them. And they all need to find someone to help so they can grow. I can show them how now." He looked down at his legs.

"Well, maybe I should stick around and help you or let them help me or something," Marvin offered. The Manager smiled.

"Marvin, you have changed. You are ready to go home now. Your family needs you like Apple's family needs him. Remember your sister?" The memory of the fire shook him back to reality.

"You're right. I HAVE to get back. But will I ever see you again?" Marvin looked at Apple and then at the Manager, and then back at his friend Apple.

"I'm sure of it!" They bumped knuckles as a handshake.

"Marvin, come on into the office for a moment," said the Manager. She had such a gentle voice with magnetic quality. It seemed to draw him so that his feet barely touched the ground. This time the door was unlocked and opened right away.

"I'd rather you left from here than from outside where all the others would notice," she smiled.

"Can I ask you something?" Marvin looked up into her face. Was it his imagination or was it glowing, just a little around her hair?

"Of course, dear," she replied, "What would you like to know?"

"Apple says that only the one who makes the directions can change them.

Are *you* the one who makes the directions?"

She looked at him for a minute and then answered gently, "Oh no, Marvin. I am only the Manager. I run the office, so to speak. The one who *makes* the directions is the OWNER." Then she turned and picked up the clipboard on the stool next to her.

"Take over for me, Porter," she ordered. "I'll be right back." The Manager motioned for Marvin to follow her. They found a quiet corner where there was a little privacy. "Are you ready to go home?" Marvin nodded, taking a last look around.

"Close my eyes?" he asked. The Manager nodded.

Chapter 20

Back Home

When he opened his eyes, Marvin was back in school. The other students were surprised to see him, but they didn't say much. It was almost time to leave for the day anyway. Marvin got his backpack and sat down at his desk quietly. Mrs. Keller looked at him but didn't say anything. When she dismissed the class, she stood by his desk and patted his shoulder gently.

"We missed you," she said.

"Thanks," he replied, so relieved that she wasn't mad at him for being such a dork. He grabbed his backpack and almost ran out of the door. He wanted to get home and make sure everything was all right.

The first thing he did was give his little sister a big hug. She started to cry, thinking he was going to hurt her. But instead of teasing her, Marvin patted her shoulder and told her NEVER to play with matches! He stuck his head in the studio room and right in the middle of a piano lesson, and told his mother that he loved her. She was so surprised that she blinked twice and said, "Are you feeling all right, honey?" Marvin just laughed.

When his family was all having dinner, Marvin asked Henry how his day had gone. Henry looked up from his mashed potatoes and said, " It was a good day, Marvin. Thanks for asking." Then his mom and Henry looked at each other and Marvin felt really smart for helping to make his parents happy. He would tell them the whole story another time. Right now he just wanted to enjoy the memories by himself, or at least until he could talk to Amy. She would understand, he thought, if anyone would.

"Do you want some apple pie, Marvin?" his mother asked as she was clearing the dinner dishes.

"Uh, no thanks, Mom," he said and went upstairs to do his homework. That would be really creepy!

The next day, Mrs. Keller asked the class to turn to page 58 in their science books. Marvin was the first to reach the correct page. He sat expectantly, waiting for further directions. Mrs. Keller was so pleased that she asked him to be the group captain. He liked that. Later, when the class was asked to walk quietly in line, Marvin stayed right where he was supposed to stay…in line. He listened carefully to hear any other important directions and was starting to feel pretty good about himself. Feeling responsible is a good feeling, he thought. Why didn't I ever get this before?

Eventually, Marvin became one of the most successful students in the class,

One day, right in the middle of a math lesson, Mrs. Keller's red cellphone rang loudly.

"Hello?" she answered. "Mm-hmm." To Marvin's surprise, and the rest of the class as well, she handed the phone to him. "It's for you, Marvin. It's the MANAGER. "

Uh-oh. What had he done now?

He took the phone and said nervously, "H-hello?"

"Hello, Marvin. I just wanted to tell you that your friend Apple would very much like to see you. He asked me to find out if you would like to come for a visit. Would you like to come back to the Directions Booth for the OFFICE PARTY?"

Marvin's face broke out in a wide smile.

"Boy, WOULD I!"

"Good! Close your eyes.

****